LEIF

AN EXISTENCE TRILOGY
NOVELLA

ABBI GLINES

—

To those of you who loved Leif and wanted him to win Pagan's heart.

Here is his side of the story

OTHER TITLES BY ABBI GLINES

In publication order by series

The Existence Series
Existence
Predestined
Leif
Ceaseless

The Rosemary Beach Series
Fallen Too Far
Never Too Far
Forever Too Far
Twisted Perfection
Simple Perfection
Take a Chance
Rush Too Far
One More Chance
You Were Mine
Kiro's Emily

The Sea Breeze Series
Breathe
Because of Low

While It Lasts
Just for Now
 Sometimes It Lasts
Misbehaving
Bad for You
Hold on Tight
Until The End

The Vincent Boys Series

The Vincent Boys
The Vincent Brothers

1. DEATH WAS STALKING HER- LEIF

It was time. I'd let her grow up normally. I'd stood back and protected her and guided her silently. Now, it was time I made her mine. The soul that the Creator had made to be her mate was gone. He'd moved away. My path was clear. Finally. I'd been waiting a lifetime for her.

I ignored the jealous glare from Kendra. She was annoying me lately. Once she'd been a good side distraction. Father had sent her to me as a form of entertainment. There were times she'd been useful, but those days were over. Kendra knew her fun had come to an end. I needed to talk to Father about removing her if she was going to cause problems. Nothing was going to stand in my way now.

I sat down in the empty seat beside Pagan. The excuse to be near her had been rehearsed in my head for over a year, when I'd started planning a way to ease into her life. She didn't like me much. Once this amused me, but now it worried me. I needed her to like me. She was my world. She always had been.

"Hey, Pagan, Mr. Yorkley said I needed to come talk to you." Pagan stared at me wide eyed. The shock in her expression was adorable. I'd been waiting to finally speak to her knowing that this time, she'd remember me.

The shock was quickly replaced with an annoyed frown. Not what I'd hoped for, but from what I could tell, she really didn't like me. Nervously, I rubbed my hands on the knees of my jeans wondering if I should have taken another route to get close to her. No, questioning my plan now was a bad idea. I had to make this work. "Uh, um, well," I began, "I mean, that is, I need some help in Speech. It isn't my thing and Mr. Yorkley said you were the one to talk to about getting some assistance."

"This is the first day of school. How can you need help already?" she asked. I forced myself to look at her, even though the disdain in her eyes was painful to witness. She wasn't buying into my excuse. This wasn't something I'd planned for.

"Um, yeah, I know,, but I, well, that is Mr. Yorkley and I know I'm going to struggle," I explained. Should I tell her about my "dyslexia" now or later? Leif Montgomery, quarterback, wouldn't be that open. He'd want to keep his cool persona. I had to remember to play the part. If this was going to work, I couldn't let her see me too clearly this soon.

"Why do you both think you'll struggle? Surely you're not afraid to speak out loud in class."

I wanted to tell her everything. I couldn't keep looking at her and reply properly. I turned my gaze away to stare straight ahead before answering. "No, that's not it," was the only response I could come up with. Real smooth.

"I don't really know why you need my help. It's really simple. You write speeches about the topics assigned and then give them orally. Simple, basic, no fancy strings or hard equations." Her dislike for me was so obvious in her tone. What had I ever done to her to make her hate me so much? I thought I was a nice guy. Everyone else liked me. Why not her?

"It isn't so easy for me." I started to say more and stopped. This wasn't going like I'd hoped. I needed to think this through. "Never mind, forget I asked." Without another glance back at her, I stood up and walked away. I'd completely screwed that up. For over ten years, I'd been waiting for the moment when I would speak to her and know that she would remember it tomorrow.

"I don't understand why you want her so badly. She's a complete bitch." Kendra caught up to me as I stalked down the hallway as far away from my debacle in the cafeteria as I could.

"Shut up, Kendra. I'm not in the mood," I growled picking up speed.

"Testy, testy. Not attractive, my prince," she replied with an amused tone.

"You're pushing it," I threatened as I reached my locker.

"She's uptight, Leif. Breaking through her wall of ice is going to be impossible."

Jerking my locker door open, I reached for my gym bag. "Leave me alone," my words left me as the eerie presence of Death crept through the halls. Kendra felt it too. She stiffened and took a step closer to me. Who was he after? No one's soul had left their body.

"Do you feel him?" Kendra whispered. The awe in her voice was obvious.

"Yeah," I replied, searching the halls for a sign of him. But I saw nothing. Slowly, the feeling left and I took a deep breath. He was gone.

"That was Dankmar, wasn't it?" Kendra asked staring up at me.

Nodding my head, I slammed my locker.

"Why was he here?"

"I have no idea, Kendra. He's Death. He can go wherever he wants to go. Just back off me, okay?"

I stepped around her and headed for the locker room. Maybe I could get some peace and quiet in there.

Death was stalking her. Anger, fear, and helplessness battled inside me. Should I go ask my father what to do? Would he know the answer to this? We'd saved her from Death once already. Why was he back? How many times would Death come for her? She was only seventeen. I had to find a way to stop this.

I couldn't get close enough to her house without alerting Death that I was near. He would feel me and come find me. Although Death had no power over me, crossing him wasn't something I wanted to do. Did he know it was me who kept her alive all those years ago when he'd come to take her soul? Had he figured it out? Was he coming to right a wrong?

"Ghede!" I called out into the darkness, knowing my father would come at the sound of my voice. I didn't come to him often for help. I preferred to keep my distance from his life in Vilokan. The Voodoo afterlife would be my final dwelling once Pagan was mine. But right now, I wanted to be close to her. Vilokan felt so dark and lonely without her with me.

"Whut do I need da fix now, huh?" Father asked as he stepped out of the darkness. The two small orange tips of his cigarettes were the only light around us.

"Dankmar is stalking Pagan. Again," I explained forcing myself not to begin pacing. Father hated it when I paced.

"Is dat so? Whut dat gurl done to send de Death afta her again?" Father pulled the cigarettes from his mouth with two of his long slender fingers and blew rings of smoke into the air before looking back at me. "Dis jus mean you got to take her now, huh? Dat all it means."

"I can't take her yet. She hates me. I don't know why, but she does. I need to make her love me before I take her to Vilokan. If she doesn't love me, she will never accept her fate."

Father shook his head and waved the hand holding the cigarettes toward Pagan's house. "You wan de Death to take her? Jus take de gurl and be done wit it. De fun is de sex, not de love."

I wanted to roar in frustration. This was not the helpful words I'd been hoping for. But then again, my father believed that sex, parties, and rum were the most important things in life. "I need her love. I've worked too damn hard to win her trust over the years. I've protected her. Met her needs. I've *trained* her. I need her love. Can't you understand that?"

Father sighed and placed the cigarettes back in his mouth, then shook his head. "You don make no sense, son. I wilt do whut I can. But if'n it's de love you need, den get it. Soon."

"I'm trying. I approached her today. I'm going to do my best. I just need more time." Tomorrow I needed a new plan. I had to make her see there was more to me than a popular football player. Stupidly, I'd thought making myself wanted among her peers would win her heart. I should've known better. Pagan wasn't shallow.

Father was gone, leaving me standing in the darkness alone once more. He was no help. Needing her love wasn't something he would ever understand. My parents' relationship had absolutely nothing to do with love. Why was I so different from them?

Lifting my eyes back to the direction of Pagan's house, I waited for him to leave. I would not let Death leave with her soul. I had to do something to protect her without alerting him. But what?

She was waiting on me outside the door to the only class we shared, Chemistry. I could feel her anxiety as she stood there. This was a good sign. At least she was coming to me because I was still unsure how to approach her again.

Stepping out into the hallway, my joy at having her waiting to speak with me was diminished by the fact Death stood somewhere nearby. I couldn't see him, but I could feel his icy cold presence.

"Um, Leif, could I talk to you a minute?" she asked. As much as I wanted to make this easy on her, I knew I couldn't. Death knew I wasn't human. I didn't want to alert him to my true intentions. I leaned against the wall and crossed my arms. She nibbled her bottom lip nervously. Death moved closer to us and I fought back the cringe that crawled over me at his nearness.

"About yesterday, I'm sorry I was so rude about helping you. I did sign up to tutor for extra credit and I shouldn't have treated you the way I did," she paused and stared up at me with an anxious expression. I wanted to ease her mind, but I couldn't. Not here. Not with *him* watching and listening. "If you still want me to tutor you, I'd be happy to." She finished and I wasn't sure what the correct response was to this.

I would do whatever she allowed just to be close to her. But Dankmar was near. I kept the bored expression on my face and pretended to be thinking her offer over. When it looked like she might bolt, I replied, "Are you offering because of Mr. Yorkley? Did he make you do this?"

The frown on her face was so damn cute. One day soon, I'd be able to reach out and smooth it away with my fingertips…or lips. "I acted the way I did because I just don't like you very much. I was wrong and, honestly, I don't even know you well enough to form an opinion of you. I'm offering to help because you need it. That's what I signed up to do and that's why I'm here now."

She admitted she didn't like me. Even though that should worry me, it didn't. The simple admission made me smile. "You don't like me, huh?"

She straightened up attempting to stand taller and gave me a small shake of her head. I couldn't help but laugh. "Well, we might have to work on changing your mind. I'll see you later," I replied then turned and walked away. Leaving her alone with Dankmar so close by bothered me. But he didn't need to know I sensed him, just like he didn't need to know I intended to take Pagan's soul before he could. After all, her soul was mine.

2. DEATH WAS TALKING TO HER- LEIF

"Dat's good, son. Da gurl is right dare witin yor reach. Don worry bout de Death. De gurl's soul don mean notin to him." Father stepped out in front of me as I started walking up Pagan's sidewalk. His top hat was cocked back on his head, which meant he'd been drinking heavily and was in a very good mood.

"Thanks, but I'm already late. I don't want to get on her bad side tonight. She isn't a fan of me yet." But she would be. I was going to make sure of it.

"Jes get de gurl. You don 'ave time for anytin else. Dankmar is close on her heels." With one final ring of smoke from his lips, he disappeared. He was right, of course. I had to find a way into Pagan's heart and fast.

Pagan opened the door almost immediately. The look on her face wasn't promising. Crap. I'd pissed her off again. Flashing her my most sincere smile, I began apologizing. "I'm really sorry about this. I feel bad you're having to work around my schedule. I know seven is late and, well, I'm sorry."

Her anger vanished and the easy smile I'd hoped to see appeared on her face. She was beautiful.

"That's okay. Go ahead and sit at the table and I'll get us something to drink. Do you like root beer?" She asked turning and walking away from me. I followed her inside. I wasn't sure I'd ever had a root beer, but that admission would sound odd.

"That's great, thanks." I replied.

Her living room wasn't new to me. I'd been here so many times before. Watching over her. Consoling her. Now, she was helping me. This time she would remember me being here. Just knowing that what we had would finally be real to her was exciting.

When she walked back into the room, I decided to ease the nervous tension surrounding us. This should be easy. "I brought the schedule for class and what all is expected in this course. I have one week before the first speech is due and it needs to be on something I feel strongly about."

She sat the soda down in front of me. "So, we need to decide what you're passionate about."

I couldn't keep the smile off my face. Passionate. That was a loaded word. One I knew a lot about.

"What?" she asked frowning.

"What I'm passionate about?" I asked still grinning.

She rolled her eyes, "You know, something you feel strongly about. Like your purpose or platform."

There was only one thing I felt passionate about, but it wasn't time I admitted that just yet. "Passionate, I like that. Let's think of something I'm passionate about."

The prissy look on her face as she puckered her lips and grabbed the notebook was just too damn cute. "Got any ideas?" she asked in a tone that said she already knew I was going to say something superficial and she was prepared to write it down.

I decided I'd throw her little know-it-all ideas for a loop. "The importance of adoption."

She began to write it down and paused. It was all I could do to keep from laughing out loud. I'd just surprised the hell out of her.

"Okay," she replied studying me closely. She wanted an explanation. Good thing I had one.

"I was adopted after living in foster homes for five years. I'd given up hope that I would get a family by the time I turned nine because most people want babies. I was given a chance most nine-year-old foster kids only dream of."

Her eyes widened in shock, "Oh, wow, I had no idea. I, uh, can see why this would be an important topic for you."

The expression on her face switched from surprise, to confusion then to what looked liked sadness. I hadn't meant to make her sad. I'd just wanted to redeem myself somehow. She thought so little of me already.

"You did hear the part where I got adopted, right?" I asked softly with an easy smile in hopes of cheering her up. "You look so distraught. I thought maybe you missed the happy ending."

"I'm sorry. It's just, well, I wasn't expecting that. You kind of surprised me."

I leaned back in my chair. "It seems to me that you've got a lot of ideas where I'm concerned. You sure have put a lot of thought into someone you don't like very much." The instant blush on her cheeks told me that I'd made some progress. If I could show her I wasn't the guy she thought I was, then I had hope that she'd love me back someday. Preferably soon. "Who knows, Pagan, you might like me before this is over."

She was warming up to me. From the way her eyes followed me down the hall and studied me from across the cafeteria, I knew her feelings toward me were changing. Our nights spent studying were now easy. We talked and laughed with none of the awkwardness that I'd been faced with in the beginning. She wasn't nervous around me anymore. My only problem was the fact that Death was still watching her.

I could feel her gaze on me as she walked down the hallway. She wanted me to turn and look at her. The attraction was like a tingling sensation running through my body. But I couldn't. Death was near her. He was the cold barrier keeping me from saying anything to her or even meeting her gaze. He'd see me and study me too closely. I didn't want him to realize the soulless being that he was obviously dismissing was more than he assumed. I wasn't one of Hell's many servants. I was the Prince of Voodoo. Dankmar didn't need to realize that too soon. It would mess up everything.

He spoke…and Pagan heard him. What? Could she see Death too? I knew my claim on her soul allowed her to see lost souls, but could it also let her see Death as well? Listening to the guys around me talking about Friday night's game was impossible. I needed to hear what he was saying. Why was Dankmar talking to a soul? What could he possibly have to say to her? He was here to take her, or at least try to. This was not normal. I needed to speak to my father. He would understand this.

I tuned out everyone around me but Pagan. I couldn't see Dankmar. I could only feel him. I also couldn't hear him. But she could. She was speaking to him. How?

"I'm not bothered," she hissed through her teeth as she opened her locker door. What did that mean? Dammit, I needed to hear what he was saying too.

Slowly, she turned her head to look at him. He must be beside her. I still could only see her. But she was studying him closely. Was her time drawing near and he was letting her know? Didn't he normally just do that with children? Why would he be giving her a heads-up?

"Staring at them will only make things worse. Ghede would advise against making a scene," Kendra's icy tone reminded me to speak with Father again about getting rid of her. She wasn't helping things. She'd grown attached to me. That had never been the plan.

"This isn't your business, Kendra," I reminded her in a hard voice. If she didn't step out of my way, I would remove her myself.

"I wonder if he's as sexy as everyone says," she purred.

"Who says Dankmar is sexy?" An alarm went off in my head. Was Death attractive?

"Everyone who has seen him. I've heard he has the bluest eyes ever created and thick black hair that is slightly too long. His smile is always cocky and his body is built for—"

"Okay, that's enough. I don't want to hear anymore of your bullshit. He's Death. He can't be sexy." That made no sense. I watched as Pagan's expression turned soft. What was he saying to her? Was she attracted to him?

"It makes perfect sense, my prince. To ease a soul's fear at its time of death, wouldn't it be easier if the one taking their soul was easy on the eyes?"

"For a girl, maybe," I replied as Pagan turned and walked away from her locker. Death was gone. I let out a sigh of relief.

"Men, too. Beauty would ease their fears as well. Something dark and sinister would be terrifying," she went on explaining. "I've heard of others who have seen him and some who have touched him or been touched by him. It's like nothing they've ever experienced. What I'd give to have him crawl between—"

"Enough!" I stopped her from anymore of her lustful thoughts. I didn't want to hear about the sexiness of Death. I needed to find a way to keep him away from Pagan.

"Hey." Pagan said stepping back to let me inside her house. Since earlier today when I'd caught her talking to Dankmar, she'd ignored me. I'd been anxious to get here. I needed to fix whatever was wrong. We had been making progress and then…nothing.

"Hey," I replied studying her closely as I followed her over to the table. The silence wasn't good. "Safe sex," I announced hoping to get some reaction out of her. I wanted the Pagan who smiled easily up at me. This quiet, reserved Pagan who ignored me was unsettling.

She froze and gaped up at me, with her mouth slightly open and a mixture of surprise and horror in her eyes. That was more like it, some animation in her gorgeous face.

"I wish you could see your face," I said, unable to keep from laughing.

"You did say 'safe sex' then?" she asked, still looking completely confused.

I held up my paper, "The topic for this week's speech."

She let out a weak laugh. "Okay, well that was one way to announce it."

She still appeared unsure. I'd wanted to ease the tension in the room, not make her nervous. So, I tried again. "I'm hoping you're well educated on this topic because I haven't got a clue."

"What?" she squeaked in reply.

I couldn't keep from laughing again at her expression. "I'm sorry. It's just that you're so cute when you're shocked."

She froze at my words and I immediately stopped laughing. What had I said wrong?

"I think having had actual experience isn't necessary. It's basically supposed to be about your beliefs on the subject or the importance of it." The tightness in her voice alarmed me. She was embarrassed. That hadn't been my intention.

I reached over and slid my finger under her chin lifting her face up so she would have to look at me. "You're embarrassed. That's cute."

My words once again didn't get the reaction I'd been hoping for. Her annoyed expression was back. "Please stop saying I'm cute. It's kind of insulting."

Insulting? What? I dropped my hand from her chin and tried hard to figure out how that was insulting. Nothing came to mind. "How's that insulting?"

Pagan shrugged, "It just is. No one wants to be cute. Puppies are cute." She didn't make eye contact with me. Instead, she started reading my notes.

"Well, you definitely don't look like a puppy," I replied with a chuckle. I'd always thought I was good with females. Pagan was proving me wrong.

"Well, that's something at least." She replied in a clipped tone. "Okay, so what are the three main reasons you believe safe sex is important?" She was trying to change the subject. I didn't want to change the subject. "Are you not sure?" she asked.

I didn't say anything. I needed to figure out how to fix my latest screw up. "Um, okay, what about teenage pregnancy? That's a good point. No one needs to become a parent while they're still a kid." She continued as if I had responded.

She began writing in my notebook determined that this conversation was over.

"Your feelings are hurt," I said as the realization came to me. "I didn't mean to say something to hurt your feelings," I assured her.

She still wouldn't look at me, "It's fine. Let's get working on your essay."

Staring down at the paper, I replied, "Teenage pregnancy is definitely one reason."

"Okay, so what about STDs?" she suggested, writing it down before I could respond. This wasn't getting us anywhere. She was still upset.

"That's another good one." I agreed.

I reached over and took the notebook from her. We were going to settle this. I didn't like knowing I'd hurt her feelings. I adored her. If only I could tell her exactly how much. "Sorry, but I couldn't think of any other way to get your attention." Her silence allowed me to continue. "You aren't just cute. Yes, you make cute faces and do cute things, but you aren't just cute." Had I said too much?

"Okay," she whispered. That was enough for now. I couldn't say more or I'd give myself away.

I slid the notebook back to her, "Now, let's see...what about the fact that using a condom takes away from the pleasure, should we discuss that?"

She began choking on her soda and I patted her gently on the back trying hard not to laugh. "Again, you do a lot of cute things, but you aren't just cute."

3. DEATH BROKE THE RULES- LEIF

"I don't have time for this now, Kendra. I told you last night that if you keep this up, I *will* have Ghede remove you. I thought you liked the attention of the human boys. You want to stay here? Then leave me alone. Back away. I don't need you here. All I have to do is tell my father and you'll be back in Vilokan. Do you want to be back under Ghede's sexual beck and call? Hmm? Didn't think so."

"I didn't do anything wrong last night. I thought you'd like to know that Death *is* here to take Pagan's soul. Her time is up, again. You go and get all pissy about missing your study date with her, but the info I had was kind of important."

She was right, of course. Pagan's soul was of the utmost importance. If Death was here to take it, then I needed to get ready.

"Now, play nice, my prince. I was just doing my job," she cooed reaching up and running a hand through my hair. Kendra really couldn't take a hint. "You sure coming over last night wasn't a big deal? I would hate to mess things up with you and your girlfriend."

Damn, she was going to screw things up for me with Pagan if she didn't shut up. The last thing Pagan needed to hear was that I had claimed her as my girlfriend. She'd be furious. "You know she isn't my girlfriend, Kendra. Stop calling her that. You'll start talk." The pleased smile that came over Kendra's face confused me. What had I said that would cause her to smile? The girl was insane.

"You spend a lot of time at her house and she's always looking at you." I was sure the people around us could hear her.

I needed to do something. Say something to fix this. Pagan did not need to hear this from someone else. I hadn't progressed that far with her. I needed to build her trust first. So, I glared down at Kendra and said the only thing that would shut everyone's gossip up. "She's my tutor and no, she isn't looking at me. You're just being paranoid when you have no reason to be."

Kendra's voice dropped to a whisper so low only I would be able to hear it. "Oops, my prince. Bad move."

"You sure she knows she isn't your girlfriend because it looks like she is stalking you?" Kendra purred and her gaze was directed over my shoulder.

If Pagan was standing behind me, I was going to extinguish Kendra with my bare hands. Turning around, my horror was complete when I found Pagan's hurt eyes taking in the scene she thought she'd just witnessed. The red splotches on her cheeks told me more than I feared. *Fuck.* What had Kendra done? I needed to do something. But what?

"Oh, uh, Pagan. I was going to come find you and explain about last night," I began.

Pagan nodded stiffly and held out a paper toward me. "Thought you might need this."

I reached out to take it, staring down at it and trying to figure out what she had for me. But as soon as I took it from her, she turned to walk away. "Wait, I was going to call you last night. I just got tied up. Thanks," I held up the paper in my hands as I realized she'd finished my speech for me.

Kendra slipped her arm inside my arm, "That's not true, Leif, I never tied you up."

I was going to kill her. Voodoo spirit or not, she was going to die. Grabbing Kendra's hand, I ripped it off my body and slung her backward before taking off after Pagan.

"Pagan," I called out to her.

Slowly, she turned around and faced me, "Yes?"

"Look, about last night, I'm really sorry. I hadn't expected you to finish the speech for me. I messed up and I was going to take the bad grade. I should've called, but—"

She shook her head, "It's not a big deal. However, from now on, would you please let me know in advance when you won't be able to make it to the appointed time for your session? Now, if you'll excuse me." The cold clipped sound of her voice felt like ice water through my veins. *No.* This could not be happening. I'd come so far with her.

"Pagan, wait, please." I begged chasing after her.

She stopped, paused, then turned back around to level me with a glare so hard I knew I'd ruined everything. "What?"

"I was coming over and Kendra called." I started.

"I don't care. Just call next time, please," she snapped, then spun back around and walked away. I wanted to go after her and beg her not to go. But what could I say to make this better?

I followed quietly after her. I needed to make sure she was going to be okay. There had been unshed tears in her eyes. It ripped me apart thinking about her hurting. The idea that she was going to cry made me want to roar in frustration.

She didn't go to her classroom. Instead, she headed for the parking lot. I stopped short when I saw a dark figure appear by her side. I knew it was Dankmar. I could feel his presence. This was it. Her death was near. She wasn't in love with me, but she had feelings for me. That would have to be enough. Because when her body died, I was going to be there to take her soul.

But her death didn't happen…

Instead, Death broke the rules. Why? It had been Pagan's time to die, again. But this time, it hadn't been me that saved her soul. Death had saved her. I backed away from the wreck scene as Death cuddled Pagan safely in his arms. Her soul was weak and trying to release, but Dankmar refused to allow it. This wasn't right. It was his job. He couldn't just choose not to take her. Could he? His cold glare lifted to meet mine. He knew I was near. A possessive gleam startled me. What did that mean? Did Death know of my claim on her soul? Was he challenging me? Did he…did he want…Pagan, too? Shaking my head, I backed away. No. That couldn't be it. That wasn't right. Death didn't care for souls. I should talk to Father about this, but first I needed to get back to school. She'd be in the hospital soon and I needed to be there when she woke up.

The sound of an ambulance was the last thing I heard before I left her there in Death's arms.

"Listen here, Leif Montgomery, I don't care who you are. All I care about is the fact my best friend is lying in that hospital room lucky to be alive because *you* upset her. I don't know what you did, but this is your fault. She. Liked. You." Miranda stood like a tiny warrior pointing her finger at me with a snarl on her face. Everything she said was correct. I wasn't going to argue or even defend myself. I deserved more. I wished Wyatt would take a swing at me. I needed to feel something. Everything inside me was numb from fear.

"You aren't worthy of her. Do you hear me? *Not worthy.* So stay the hell away from her. I love her. She is like my sister. If something had happened to her—" Miranda stopped and sobbed loudly. Wyatt was instantly at her side pulling her into his arms. He wasn't happy with me either. The worried frown on his face as he held Miranda in his arms told me he would have words with me when Miranda wasn't around.

"I know I don't deserve her," I replied in a low whisper. I'd protected her from the time I'd saved her soul from Death. But now, when she needed me most, I'd sent her away right back into Death's embrace. Why he hadn't taken her soul, I couldn't figure out. It didn't make sense.

"Why Kendra? She is so, so, ugh," Miranda hissed.

I couldn't argue with that. "It wasn't anything like you think. I'm in love with Pagan. Kendra is an annoying pest that can't accept I've moved on."

Miranda straightened up and turned her full attention on me. "You love Pagan?" she asked with awe in her voice.

I'd said that aloud. Well, it was time I admitted it. "Yes, but please don't tell her I said that. Right now, she isn't ready to hear it."

Miranda nodded and a small smile touched her lips, "I agree. She doesn't need to hear that right now. But you're going to need a lot of luck to get back in her good graces. Considering you almost—" Miranda stopped and her eyes filled up with tears again. I didn't need to ask her to know what she was thinking.

"I know. I intend to do everything I can to win her forgiveness."

Death was singing to her? What in the *hell* was that about? I came by everyday. I brought her the foods she requested. I spent time with her just the way I'd always wanted. We laughed. It was perfect…but at night he was coming to her. He was singing to her as she slept. The lyrics he sang weren't words the lord of Death should be directing at anyone. Clinching my fist to keep from walking into her room and demanding he leave, I listened to the words.

"The life I walk binds my hands,
it makes me take things that I don't understand.
I walk this dark world unknowing of what they hold true,
forgetting the me I once knew,
until you.
The life I walk eternally was all I knew,
nothing more held me here to this earth,
until you.
I feel the pain of every heart I take,
I feel the desire to replace all that I have grown to hate.
Darkness holds me close but the light still draws my empty soul.
The emptiness where I used pain to fill the hole
no longer controls me, no longer calls me
because of you."

Dread ran through me as the meaning of those words sank in. Dankmar was attached to Pagan. He'd kept her alive because he *felt* something for her. She was mine. I'd been there. I'd saved her and molded her. Death was *not* going to take her away from me. I couldn't tell Father. He'd demand that I just take her. She wasn't ready for that yet. Not now. She was so close to feeling for me something deeper than friendship. I needed her love. I had to win her love. When I took her from this life, I wanted her to go willingly. Dankmar would not stand in my way. She didn't know who he was. She couldn't. If she did, she'd be terrified. Pagan would not fall in love with Death. I knew her well enough to know that she'd never accept who he really was.

4. A TASTE OF HEAVEN- LEIF

"If you aren't ready to start on my speech, I'm not in a hurry," I whispered in Pagan's ear as she cuddled up against my side. She sighed and pressed closer to me as we sat on the couch. We were supposed to be watching a movie, but that wasn't happening. I'd been doing algebra equations in my head all evening to keep my mind from dwelling on the warmth of Pagan's body, the honeysuckle scent in her hair, and the fact her hand was just above the waist of my jeans. Her other hand was clasped firmly in mine. Being this close was like a taste of heaven. The problem was my body wanted to have a larger bite. Preferably with Pagan on her back and me pressing down on her. *No!* I had to get a grip.

My cell phone rang causing Pagan to squeal and cling to me. "It's my phone, not the fire alarm. Jeesh, you're jumpy tonight." I teased reaching into my pocket and pulling it out. The number was private which meant it was my father.

"Hello?"

"Death is jest outside de gurl's house. Leave," Father replied in my ear. I hadn't felt Death's presence. Why was Father calling me about this? I wasn't ready to leave. Pagan was mine.

"I'm at Pagan's right now....I realize that, but I'm busy....We haven't finished it yet."

"Don argue wit me. Leave. Now."

"Okay, I'm on my way," I replied knowing arguing with my father was pointless. He had his reasons. I wasn't going to go far when I left.

Death had been here almost every night for weeks. I didn't understand it, but I dealt with it.

"That was my dad. He needs me to ride with him to drop mom's car off at the mechanic's. They're going to work on it first thing in the morning. He can't go to bed until he has dropped it off and he's beat after working a double shift at the station." I lied.

Pagan frowned sitting up straight, "Oh, yeah, um, go on. We can work on the speech tomorrow."

Something was bothering her. I did not want to leave her. Ever. "You look uptight. I hate to leave you all wound up."

She forced a smile that didn't meet her eyes. "I probably just need some sleep."

Leaning down, I captured her mouth with mine and nipped gently on her bottom lip. Her mouth opened immediately and I slipped my tongue inside needing a taste. Leaving her was never easy. Having her warmth and taste on my lips would give me something to hold close until tomorrow morning.

Pagan pressed up against me and her breast brushed against my chest. All good intentions I may have had flew out the window as a hungry moan escaped my chest. Shifting, I laid Pagan back on the couch and came over her quickly taking her sweet swollen lips again.

Her legs parted and I eased down between them tucking my body as close to hers as it had ever been. The warmth cradling my hips sent a shiver of pleasure through my body. I needed more. Slipping my hands under her shirt, I reached the bottom edge of her bra.

"No," that one word brought me back to reality. Slowly, I took my hand out from under her shirt and sat up pulling her with me. My breath was choppy and my heart was racing. I'd been so close to touching her. My erection was pressing against the zipper of my jeans causing a small amount of pain. Just enough to remind me that I needed to get the hell out of here.

"Wow," I managed. "I'm sorry, I got carried away," my eyes fell to the bottom of her shirt that was still bunched up from where my hand had crept underneath it. The flat smooth skin of her stomach mocked me and I winced as my hard-on jerked against the metal pressing into it.

"Don't apologize. We just needed to stop. Your dad is waiting."

My father. Damn. I'd forgotten. Standing up, I grabbed my jacket and books. "Are you going to be okay until your mom gets home?"

Pagan smiled at me and nodded. I started to walk back over to her and get one more taste of her lips, but I didn't. Instead, I forced myself to walk out the door.

Dank Walker may be ignoring Pagan at school, but Death was still watching her. I didn't understand his actions, but as long as he continued to hurt her and push her away, I would stand back and let him send Pagan running into my arms.

5. SHE WAS MY CREATION- LEIF

They were letting him *keep* her? What were they thinking? Death couldn't just have a soul. This was asinine. He was Death, dammit. He removes the soul. He doesn't keep the soul. Pagan wrapped her arms tightly around Dankmar's neck as if he was a life preserver and she was drowning. Once, that had been me. I'd been the one she ran to. I had been her safe place. She may not remember it, but every moment in her life I had been there. It had been my arms that held her. It had been my words that soothed her. Always me. I'd taken my time. I'd wanted her to grow up normally. The world in which I dwelled wasn't easy. Making sure she had love and safety as she grew had been my number one priority. Father had told me to take her sooner, but I'd waited. I'd wanted her to choose me. To want me...and she had. But only for a moment.

Death's cold eyes lifted and met mine. The challenge was there. He wanted her, but did he really know her? She was my creation. I could read every expression on her face. I understood her emotions. The bright glow lit his eyes and I knew he wouldn't stand by while I explained everything to her. Pagan was in his arms. That was where she wanted to be, for now. But I held all the memories that would change things. Finding a way to get close enough to her to feed the lost memories of our times together back into her thoughts would be difficult. Father would know how. I'd go seek help from him. Dankmar may be Death, but I wasn't without power. Pagan would see that there were things she needed to know before she made her final decision.

I wouldn't let her shut me out today. Not here. Not now. First, she would remember. Then, once she understood what I was to her, I would let her choose. In the end, Pagan would choose me. She had to. There wasn't going to be another choice.

"Don come in here askin' fer me da help you. Jus' take da gurl. Fuck Dankmar. Jes cause he won de gurl don mean he can 'ave her. Dat ain't whut de rules say. De gurl's soul is yers. Now, take it." My father, Ghede, the Voodoo lord of the dead, stood up scowling at me as the redheaded female spilled from his lap onto the floor. Without even a glimpse back at her to see if she was alright, Father grabbed his two signature cigarettes and lit them with a simple snap of his fingers. The woman on the floor scrambled to pull the low cut top of her dress back over her bare breasts. The nervous mannerisms of her movements caught my attention. That wasn't normal. Most of my father's harem would have continued to lay sprawled out on the floor with their bare chest in clear view of anyone who decided to look their way. Frowning, I noticed the light pink in her cheeks and jerked my gaze back to Father's.

"She's alive?" I asked, unable to mask the horrified expression on my face.

Father chuckled and shifted his dark gaze to the woman while taking a long puff on his cigarettes. "I get bored. De chit shouldn't ave messed wit de Voodoo. De blush in her cheeks is nice, heh? I lak dis one."

The complete disregard to the woman's life didn't surprise me. Father never was one to care much about life. He enjoyed the death of a follower. Taking a soul inside its human body wasn't something he did. Unless they allowed him to by practicing Voodoo rituals that opened themselves up to his interference.

"What of her body? Will you just keep it too?"

Father flashed a wicked smile toward the woman whose rapidly beating heart I could hear from across the room. "I lak de body."

Stupid woman. She was now Ghede's new toy until he was bored with her. Shaking my head, I couldn't think about that right now. I had my own set of issues. "Father, please, just tell me what to do. Dankmar has her. She wants him. How do I make her remember? He protects her and I can't get anywhere near her."

Father reached up and adjusted his top hat before pulling the cigarettes from his mouth and leaning forward across the desk. "Dankmar is Death. He can't always be dere wit de gurl."

Dankmar had a job to do. If he was with Pagan during the day, then...that left the night.

"I go to her while he's working," I said aloud and my father nodded his head and slipped the cigarettes back between his lips.

"Yes. Give de memories to her while she sleeps."

In her dreams. Perfect.

6. It's almost time- Leif

I waited, ready to catch her if she fell. My Pagan was always up to something dangerous. I spent more time keeping her alive than I did comforting her. It was rare that she cried. But then, I never allowed something to upset her for long. If a frown appeared on her perfect face, I found a way to make her smile. Today, she wasn't exactly making me very happy. Seeing her climb up a tree was difficult. Every small slip of her foot caused me a moment of panic.

Just as I'd feared, her foot slipped and this time my brave girl couldn't catch herself in time. Stepping up to the tree until I stood directly under her, I held out my arms ready to once again catch her from falling out of this tree. It would be the third time this summer.

"Umph, got you," I assured her as I stared down at her tightly closed eyes. Her eyelids blinked rapidly before opening and gazing up at me. The confusion in her eyes when she saw me was always so painful. I hated that she couldn't remember me. That she couldn't remember the times we'd spent together.

"Uh," she mumbled in confusion as she shifted her eyes from my face to the tree.

"What were you doing up there? That was too high." I told her this every time. It never did any good, but I kept trying. Maybe one day it would stick.

"Um, I uh...did you catch me?" she asked in that familiar surprised voice.

"Yeah. Why else do you think you're not lying on the ground with a few broken bones?" I asked trying not to laugh. She didn't like it when I laughed at her. It was as if she knew she was missing out on some important piece of information and she hated being out of the loop.

When she began to wiggle in my arms, I stood her up carefully. The curious expression on her face soothed some of the ache in my chest. She remembered me…at least her heart did. I could see it in her eyes. She was trying so hard to open up those memories.

"Where'd you come from?"

She always asked me this, "Just around. Saw you climbing too high and came over to see if you needed help."

"Do I know you?" she asked watching my face for any sign of a clue.

"I wish you did, but you don't. Not yet. It isn't time." I bit back my words. I shouldn't have said that. I needed to be more careful with the things I said to her. Even if she would forget me by the end of the day.

"What do you mean?" she asked with a frown.

"Pagan Moore, get your butt over here if you're going to get a sneak peek at my tree house before the boys get here." Her friend, Wyatt, called to her from the street. He wouldn't be able to see me. That would confuse her. It was time I left, for now.

Slowly, I let the memory fade as I watched Pagan's sleeping form toss and turn. This time she wouldn't forget. She hadn't connected me to the boy in her dreams just yet. But she would. With one last promise, I whispered into her ear, *"It's almost time."* Before leaving her alone to wake up.

"De gurl won choose you over Dankmar. Jes take her," Father stood in the backyard of Pagan's house.

"She's remembering, Father. I need time," I glanced back up at her window and watched as she stood staring at the tree. The memories would change things. They had to.

"De memories, dey wan be 'nough." He drawled over the cigarettes hanging from his mouth.

"They will," I growled in frustration.

"De Death draws near. Leave me. Ahm gonna talk da him," Father demanded. The dark coal black eyes met mine and I knew there was no arguing with him. He'd speak to Dankmar. There was no way I could stop him. But I wasn't going to go too far. I wanted to hear what Dankmar said. Would Father tell him that Pagan's soul was mine? If so, I had to be here.

Stepping back into the woods I waited. I knew the moment Dankmar felt my father's presence. The threat rolling off his form was impossible to miss. Pagan kissed him and I closed my eyes unable to watch.

Then she was back inside the house and Dankmar was turning to face my father.

"What do you want with Pagan?" he asked quietly, but the hard edge to his voice was terrifying.

"She belongs to me." Father replied without backing down. The Dankmar that had walked the hallways of the high school had been so nonthreatening that I'd forgotten at times the true power of the Death Lord. Now, seeing him like this, I cringed backing up against the tree behind me.

"No. She doesn't." Dankmar replied taking a step toward Father. I wasn't surprised when my father took a step backwards. The winds had stilled in Death's presence and all living things had fled his presence. A dark growl encased the silence.

"De gurl is marked as a restitution. Her mama made de deal. She know de cos."

"Pagan Moore is mine. Leave her alone. You've never crossed me before, but I can assure you that a Voodoo spirit lord is no match for me. You know this."

For the first time in my existence, I watched as my father's body tensed in fear. He'd pushed Death too far. "But de restitution mus be made."

"*Not* with Pagan it doesn't. Whatever deal you had with her mother is with her mother. Pagan had nothing to do with this."

"You'd of nevah known her if I hadn't healed her. You'd of taken her soul whilt she lay curled up dying as a child. It's me who don lak to see chilren die. You don care who you take. She's alive 'cause of me. She's meant for me purpose. I saved her for me son. He's watched over her all dese years." I stood frozen as Father explained to Dankmar exactly what we'd done all those years ago. The violent expression on his face told me all I needed to know. He wasn't going to let her go. He may extinguish me and my father, but he would not let Pagan go.

"Leave her or deal with me."

"De gurl wilt have to choose or ahm takin' my payment in udder forms. I got de right," the tremble in Father's voice was unmistakable.

"Fine! Let her choose," Dankmar roared.

Without waiting to see what happened, I fled.

7. He was bound to love you- Leif

Either Dankmar or the transporter always stayed close to Pagan's side. Thanks to them, she was terrified of me. The orange flames in her eyes caused by my nearness were the only comfort I received from being in her presence. I hated knowing she was scared of me. *Me!* The reason she was alive. Her source of comfort.

I was going to fix that. If everything went as planned, she'd be rushing out of that door any moment. Hopefully, heartbroken and ready to listen to me.

As if on cue, the backdoor flew open and Pagan's tear streaked face immediately made me question my actions. I didn't like seeing her cry. I'd set Dankmar up. A Voodoo spirit in the form of a very attractive female made Pagan think she was seeing something that really wasn't happening.

"I'll take you home," I said from a distance. I needed her to come to me.

She spun around and stiffened immediately as her eyes found me in the darkness. Her hands lifted to wipe the tears rolling down her face. I ached to go wipe the tears for her. Before I could move and screw up my perfectly developed strategy to get her alone, she took a step toward me.

"Sure, thanks, Leif. I could use a ride."

That was not what I had been expecting. This was just too easy. Opening the passenger side door, I stepped back and let her climb inside. Touching her was too much, too soon. First, she needed to see that I was still the same boy she'd once cared for. Not the evil Voodoo Prince she was told to fear. Once she was safely inside, I closed the car door and took one last glance back at the door she'd come through. Dankmar was drawing closer. I wouldn't have time to take her away safely. He'd find her. I had to take her to my home much sooner than expected.

I knew apporting Pagan was dangerous. But then, I figured Death protected her body and I owned her soul. How bad could it be? She'd been sleeping since we arrived. Her body hadn't been able to handle it as well as I'd hoped. Stirring in her sleep, she mumbled, "Dank," then whimpered. I hated him.

"Shhhh, it's okay, Pagan. Don't get all worked up. I've got you." I assured her brushing the hair back from her face.

"Leif?" she whispered.

"Yes, I'm here," I replied loving the shiver that coursed through her body.

"Where am I? Why can't I open my eyes?" I could hear her uncertainty.

"You're with me for now. Where you belong. Where you've always belonged. You've been mine since the moment I chose you when we were both just children. And as for your eyes, they'll open soon enough. Your human body had difficulty dealing with the travel and for that I'm sorry."

"I don't understand." She replied. No, she wouldn't understand. Not now. There was so much I had to tell her. But not while she was like this.

"Just rest. You'll feel better soon."

She slowly drifted back to sleep. Carrying her to my bed, I laid her down. I'd let her sleep this off a little while longer. Father needed to know I'd brought her here. It was better if I explained things to him first. Just in case Death descended on us sooner rather than later.

After speaking with Father I hurried back to check on Pagan. Having her here, in Vilokan, in my bed, felt complete. Finally. Although, I couldn't keep her. Not yet. I just needed to talk to her. Get her to understand. It had been impossible to speak with her any other way. Dankmar was always with her or that…that…annoying as hell transporter who I didn't want to cross. The blonde transporter was one scary female.

"You're awake," I said smiling as I entered the room and found Pagan awake standing in the center of the room.

"Where are we?" She asked in a shaky voice.

"My place. You like it?" I quipped hoping to ease her anxiety.

"Why am I here, Leif?"

"Because you belong to me." I shouldn't have blurted it out like that. Bad timing.

She took a step toward me and a fierce expression had taken over her worried frown. "I don't belong to you, Leif. I'm not a possession. I'm a person. Please take me back home."

Oh, hell no. The fury at the thought of her belonging to Dankmar began churning inside me. "So that *Dankmar* can have what I created? I don't think so, Pagan." I had to calm down. She'd fear me if I lost it. She was saying what she believed to be true. I had to get a hold of myself.

"You see, he was bound to love you. You're different. He saw that. But what he failed to explain is that you're different because I made you different. Not him. Not fate. Me. Everything about you has been molded into my creation. You were chosen for me." Holding out my hand, I took a step toward her, "It's okay, trust me. My touch would never harm you."

Pagan shook her head frantically and began backing away from me. Why? All I'd ever done was protect her. Why did she have to see me as something dark, something evil? I loved her. "Have I ever hurt you, Pagan? Listen to your soul. It knows where it belongs. The fire flashing in your eyes right now is your soul reaching for me." I closed the distance between us, "Give me your hand."

"Please, Leif, take me home. I just want to go home," she pleaded.

Dropping my hand back to my side, I gave up on trying to get her to touch me. We were going to have to work on the trust issue.

"What must I do to make you trust me? You trust Death without question. *Death*, Pagan. He is Death. How can you trust a creation meant to take souls from earth and not trust me? I've never let you get hurt. I've never left you alone. But he shows up and you fall mindlessly under his spell. What did he do to deserve you? He didn't save your life. He would've taken your soul when you were a kid. Left your mother grieving the loss of her child and not thought of it again. It's what he does." I was desperate to get her to understand.

"But why did you save me?" her question didn't surprise me. She never did understand how incredibly special she was.

"I'm not your darkest dream, Pagan. I may walk in the darkness, but I saw a life worth saving and I chose it. My father chose it. He agreed you were meant for me. Now it's up to you to accept that the life you have always lived is coming to an end. It's past time. You were supposed to die that day on the road and when Death came, I was to take your soul instead. You would've trusted me. Your soul and my spirit are one. But Death broke the rules." The frustration in my chest became a growl and I stalked away from her. Growling wasn't exactly something that would ease her fear of me. I stopped in front of one of the many candles I'd used to light the room. "I'd become lax in my judgment. I knew Death was with you, but I believed he was doing what he does when he takes a special interest in a soul, preparing you. Instead, the fool was falling in love with you."

Holding my hand over the flame I grabbed the warmth and energy flickering against my palm and held it tightly before turning back around to look at her. "I may not control Death, but I do control the dead. Those who made less than intelligent choices on earth. They walk in the darkness under my father's command. Under my command. I need someone to fill the loneliness. You've been my companion for over fifteen years now even if you don't realize it. But your memories will slowly return. You'll see that you do, in fact, belong to me."

Pagan shook her head as her eyes focused on the ball of fire in my palm. "You're just going to take me from earth? What about my mother? I can't just leave her."

No. That wasn't what I planned to do. Shaking my head, I extinguished the flame in my palm and walked back over to stand in front of her.

"I'll take you back soon. She won't even realize you were gone. I just needed a place where I could talk to you. To explain, without," unable to control the distaste over her affections for Dankmar, I snarled, "that stupid transporter or Dankmar continuously botching my attempts."

The sigh of relief in her voice told me she'd once again thought the worst of me. "You were worried I would hold you prisoner? Come on, Pagan, you know me better than that. When have I not made sure you were happy? When have I ever intentionally hurt you? Never." I reached out and took her hand in mine. When she didn't snatch it out of my grasp, I pulled her beside me.

"What is it you want to talk to me about?" she asked studying me. She was calmer now. The rapidly beating sound of her heart had eased.

"That's better. Your heart has slowed down. I don't like having you scared. I never want you to fear me," I squeezed her hand in reassurance of my sincerity. "Come for a walk with me, please. We can talk while I show you around." I reached for the stone wall that I knew would open up onto Bourbon Street.

Pagan stepped out into the warm New Orleans evening. Her eyes widened in shock as she scanned our surroundings. The bars, dance clubs, and Voodoo shops were all lit up against the darkness of the night. Tap dancing kids, drunken men, and topless women all claimed her attention as if it were a play being performed just for her. The familiarity of the scene in front of us suddenly seemed vulgar as I watched Pagan take in the lewd behavior I'd grown up amidst. I didn't want her watching anymore. It was all wrong. She didn't belong. She was too good, too pure.

"Come on, Pagan, you've got your eyeful. Let's go for a ride," I replied leading her toward the buggy I'd summoned.

"We're going to ride?" she asked as I picked her up and placed her safely inside. I suddenly wanted to take her somewhere that was good enough for her. This was too dirty. It wouldn't do.

"Yep," I replied taking the seat across from her. "So, what do you think of Bourbon Street? Everything you'd ever imagined?" I wanted to make light of the inappropriate behavior I'd just forced her to witness.

"These shops, the Voodoo ones...," she asked trailing off.

Chuckling, I glanced over at one of the ridiculous shops set up to take advantage of tourists with hopes of finding a spell for true love or a skinnier waist line or revenge on their enemies. If they only knew.

"Are owned by regular people sucking the tourists dry. Not one of them hold any power. I'd guess if a real Voodoo spirit were to grace their doors, they'd close up and leave town. The real Voodoo isn't along these streets. It can only be found deep in the swamp by those chosen by the spirits to embody it.

"This is the Garden District. It's a nicer area. The most well preserved southern mansions can be found right here." I explained, relieved to be leaving the filth of my world behind us.

"What did you want to talk to me about, Leif? Why am I here?"

She was ready to talk now. Okay. We could talk. I leaned forward resting my elbows on my knees and held her gaze. "I know you understand now what your mother did. You remember all the times I've come to you in your life. You know it was me that day in the old Voodoo queen's home that removed the sickness from your body. Yes, I did it and I require, my father requires, restitution for it. All gris-gris comes with payment. Not the monetary kind like the Voodoo shop owners require. Real Voodoo requires something more. The more difficult the request, the more the payment will be. I wanted you to live Pagan. I'd watched you from the moment you arrived in New Orleans. The nurse watching over you was the granddaughter of the Voodoo queen. She brought me to see you the first day you arrived. I was fascinated with your spunk. My father was looking for my mate and I went to him with the request to have you. He said we must wait. That if it was meant to happen, then fate would play into our hands. When the doctors said you would not see another day, your mother went to the nurse and she brought you to the old Voodoo queen who summoned me." I forced myself to stop. She needed time to process all of this. I'd just been waiting so long to tell her all these things. Time was short. Dankmar would find her soon. Our time was limited and I wanted so badly to make her understand.

"A life cannot be spared for free. The cost of a life is a life. I saved your life and in doing so bought your soul. It has been mine since the day you were healed. I've been near you ever since."

The frown on Pagan's face puckered her forehead. "None of this makes sense. Why did you become human? Why did you ignore me for years? Why did you pretend with me? Why do you want me? Why can't you just let me go?"

She was ready to listen.

Then I felt his power. The life around us stilled. Not even the birds would remain in Death's presence. I'd been so close to making her understand. So damn close.

"He's here. How the hell did Dankmar get here so quickly?" Without a backward glance, I left her there. I wasn't ready to face Dankmar. He still held all the cards—her love and his authority over life.

8. HE IS DEATH. SEE HIM FOR WHO HE IS- LEIF

"If'n de gurl won come, den ahm gonna take an udder," Father informed me announcing his appearance. Standing outside the high school where I'd been following Pagan for the past three years, watching her and waiting on her, I'd thought taking her from her soul's mate would be my biggest hurdle, but her mate had made it way too easy.

"Father," I replied in greeting. "I don't want another. You know that. I want Pagan."

"De gurl needs a push in da right direction, huh?"

"You taking another soul isn't going to affect her. She won't realize that you took a soul in her place. And I'm not telling her that. It would make me appear as an even bigger monster in her eyes than I already do."

Father let out an eery chuckle, "I dinna say who woulda take her place, hmmm?"

"What is that supposed to mean?" I asked, concern at his humor jerking my thoughts off Pagan and my re-entrance into her human world.

"Ahm gonna make shur dat gurl makes da right choice. Dats all."

"What do you mean?" I asked, but it was too late. He was gone. With a frustrated sigh, I jerked my backpack up on my shoulder and headed for the front doors of the high school. Pagan wasn't scared of the boy she'd always known as a classmate. I needed to remind her that I was still that guy. Nothing had changed.

"Speaking of hotness, here comes your last drool-worthy boyfriend," Pagan's best friend since childhood whispered as I made my way toward them.

Right as I reached her locker, she closed it a little too loudly before turning to face me. I wanted to laugh at her angry glare, but I figured that wouldn't win me any points. Seeing her brave enough to be angry with me was a nice change. Anything was better than her being terrified of me.

"Leif," she mumbled. Her eyes darted everywhere but directly at me. She was so dang cute.

"Pagan, it's good to see you, too."

"What do you need?" She snapped and Miranda elbowed her a little too hard. I clinched my fist to keep from reaching out and grabbing her friend's arm and moving her away from Pagan.

"Well, I was wondering about the tutoring. I mean, now that I'm back, I need to keep up my grade and you know I can't do it without your help."

Pagan's eyes finally focused on me and went wide. That hadn't been what she was expecting me to say. Good. "Ah, well, when you *left*, I filled your spot. But I'm sure there are other tutors available if you feel you *really* need one."

"But you were so helpful. I doubt anyone else will be able to help me the way you did." Anger flashed in her pretty eyes as she pulled her backpack up her arm and stepped around me.

"I'm so sorry, Leif. I don't know what has gotten into her today," Miranda began babbling. I was affecting her. The emotion was a good thing.

"It's okay. I did leave without a word. I'm sure I have a lot of making up to do."

"Well, she has kind of moved on, ya know?" I didn't want to listen to Miranda tell me about Dank Walker and his claim on what was mine.

Brushing her off with a nod, I walked away without a word in response.

The sirens drew me from my path to the homeroom I would now be sharing with Pagan. Instead, I headed out to the backdoors and followed Pagan and Miranda who had both broken into a run toward the football field.

As I neared, I saw the field filled with emergency technicians, students, and the sounds of panicked cries drifted through the air as Miranda draped herself over Wyatt's lifeless body. Lifting my eyes, I found Dankmar standing there unnoticed by the crowd. The pain and confusion on his face told me all I needed to know.

Wyatt had been what my father's riddle was all about earlier. He'd taken Wyatt in Pagan's place. He hadn't taken just any soul, but a soul she would mourn—a soul that would get her attention.

Pagan lifted her eyes and I watched as she glared at Death. She finally understood. She didn't understand that this death was not one taken by Dankmar, but she did get a taste of what his purpose in life consisted of. He wasn't the rocker that girls fawned over. "He is Death, see him for who he is," I whispered before turning and leaving the tragedy behind me.

9. IT LOOKS LIKE IT'S JUST YOU AND ME - LEIF

"Whoa, not who I expected to see here," I said aloud in order to announce my presence. Pagan and Miranda hadn't realized they weren't alone in the cemetery. But then Pagan seemed to have her hands full with a very drunk Miranda. "And drinking?" I shifted my gaze from the bottle of wine to Pagan.

"She wanted to come here. I figured she needed some courage to face it." The annoyed snip in her voice I'd recently grown accustomed to was gone. She sounded…tired.

Being the cause of all the pain I'd watched her experience since Wyatt's death weighed heavy on my chest. Now, she looked like she was at her breaking point. "I can understand that," I replied.

Miranda scooted over and patted the spot beside her on the bench in front of Wyatt's grave. "Come sit," she instructed me with a slur.

I took the offered seat. "Here, it's good," Miranda shoved the bottle into my chest. Yeah, she'd had way too much.

"Don't mind if I do," If I drank some, maybe it would help me deal with what I was about to do. Time was running out. If I didn't get Pagan's attention tonight, it was very possible my father would take another soul—someone else close to her. I couldn't let that happen.

"Sorry I ran off today and we juslefyouthere." Miranda apologized for the episode I'd witnessed at the mall earlier. Pagan didn't respond. Instead, she reached across Miranda and took the wine bottle out of my hand.

"You've reached your limit, Miranda. Any more and you'll hate me tomorrow," Pagan said as she shoved the cork back in the bottle and set it down on the ground beside her feet.

"I was worried about you, but I saw Pagan caught up with you," I responded to Miranda.

"Yesss. Don know whatid do withouther," Miranda slurred.

"She's pretty special," I agreed leaning forward to meet Pagan's gaze.

Miranda nodded then started to lay her head on Pagan's shoulder, but missed and fell forward. I reached down and pulled her back up as Pagan did the same thing. Our hands brushed and I felt a warm jolt from the brief contact. Begging her wouldn't work, but I often wondered if times like these might just sway her vote a little bit. Maybe.

"Okay, I believe it's time for us to go home," Pagan announced standing up. "Come on, you. Let's get you to bed."

"I'll help you get her to the car," I offered.

Miranda fell forward on her knees and cackled with laughter.

"Yeah, okay, thanks," Pagan muttered.

I was more than positive that Pagan's sudden willingness to accept my help had to do with the fact Miranda was more than a little out-of-control. I reached down and picked her up under the arms. Once I had her standing up, I wrapped my arm around her waist as she began swaying and giggling. "Easy, girl," I tried to sound encouraging. It was my father's fault she was like this after all.

"Easygirl," Miranda mimicked laughing. "Bye, Wyatt, loveyousomuch," she called out as I led her back down the path toward the parking lot. The souls wandering the cemetery could sense me. They knew I saw them just as they knew Pagan did too. I dodged the ones standing in our way.

"Loveyousomuch," Miranda began to chant. As soon as I reached Pagan's car, I opened the passenger side door and eased Miranda into the seat. Then without asking, I opened the back door and climbed inside. I didn't want to give Pagan a chance to turn me down. Tonight we had to talk. She needed to *know*. If I didn't explain things to her, another soul she loved would be lost to her forever. I couldn't let that happen.

Pagan opened the opposite rear door and stuck her head in looking at me like I had lost my mind. "What do you think you're doing?" she hissed.

"I'm making sure you two get home safely," I replied with a smile I hoped was reassuring.

"Oh no, you're not. Get out!" She came close to screaming.

"Donbesomean, Pagan," Miranda chimed in from the front.

I could see the uncertainty in Pagan's frown. Finally, she rolled her eyes and slammed the door. Then she opened the driver side door and climbed in. I heard a mumbled, "Whatever," before she slammed her door. I guess that one was for good measure. In case I missed the fact she'd slammed the first door.

"Stay awake. I won't be able to get you inside if you're passed out. We don't want your Daddy coming out and finding you like this." Pagan told Miranda in a gentle scolding voice.

Miranda managed to wake up some from the droopy-eyed girl who'd been falling asleep.

"That's better, keep those eyes open," Pagan encouraged rolling down the windows. "The cold air should help and if you start to feel sick, please lean out that window and puke."

"Whose idea was it to get her wasted?" I asked already knowing the answer.

"Paaagaaans, shesosmart." Miranda replied with a giggle when it was obvious Pagan was ignoring me.

"Canwedoit agaaain to…tomorrow?" Miranda asked.

"No. Trust me, the headache you're going to have in the morning will agree with me. That was a one-time deal." Pagan replied.

When Pagan pulled into Miranda's drive, I quickly opened my door and started getting Miranda out of the car. She wasn't going to make it up that walkway and stairs without my help.

Once we reached the door, Miranda's mother opened it and Pagan stepped forward handing her mother the almost empty bottle of wine.

"She wanted to go see Wyatt's grave tonight. I took this because I felt like she would need it. I'm sorry—"

Miranda's mother held up her hand to stop any further explanation. "No, it's okay. I understand. That's not any worse than the pills I've been giving her." I could see the worry and fear in her mother's eyes and I was reminded once again of how important it was that Pagan knew. Everything. Tonight.

"Just go on home tonight, Pagan. Your mom's already called me looking for you. Her plane arrived an hour ago. I'll look after Miranda tonight." Miranda's mother informed her.

After she closed the door, I turned to look at Pagan, "Looks like it's just you and me."

10. I LIED TO YOU- LEIF

"No, it's just me and I'm going home," Pagan replied spinning around in an angry huff and stalking toward her car. I, of course, had already taken her keys.

I watched as she began frantically searching for the keys she'd left in her ignition. Opening the passenger side door, I slid quickly inside. The keys dangled from my finger as I smiled at her. That didn't win me any points. But I hadn't really expected it to. She was forcing me to do this.

Pagan snatched the keys and cranked up the car. "What do you plan on doing, Leif? Going inside and visiting with my mom? Hmmm... because more than likely Gee is going to be there shortly after I arrive and she's chomping at the bit to kick your ass."

Unfortunately, she wouldn't be going back to her house. Not tonight. Not ever. "No, Pagan, I just think you and I need to talk."

"About what? The fact you want to take my soul off to some Voodoo hereafter or the fact that you stalked me my entire life then took my memories away from me? I know! You want to talk about how you *lied* to me about everything from the very beginning and made me think you were this nice guy. Pick a topic because I'm all talked out with them all."

She didn't understand. Dankmar had made me sound so evil. She had chosen him as her light. Death as her light? How insane was that? Sighing, I rubbed my palms against my knees. "You're angry with me. I get it. I even understand it. I always expected you to be once you knew—"

"Then why do it?" She interrupted.

"Because I picked you. It was your purpose. It is your purpose. Don't you get it? You'd have died, Pagan. Died. Gone on. Gotten another life and completely lost the chance at this life. Because you were going to die. Death wasn't in love with you then. He was going to take you like he was supposed to. There was nothing anyone could do to stop him, except your mother. She could choose to hand you over to Ghede and she did. She may not have realized it, but when she begged a Voodoo doctor to save you with Voodoo magic, she gave you over to my father. So you lived. You didn't die. Death didn't take you. You got to grow up with your mother and have friendships with Miranda and even Wyatt. You got to *live*. Those were years you wouldn't have gotten had I not chosen you. This life you have now would have ended that night in the New Orleans Children's Hospital." *Ghede!* Why couldn't she just get that? Any other human would understand what she was so blinded by.

Pagan started to turn the car toward her house. I reached over and took over the steering wheel to stop her. "No. We aren't done talking."

She tried to fight me and force the car to turn, but it wouldn't, I had complete control over the direction we would be headed. We wouldn't stop until we reached the old East Gulf Bridge. Then we wouldn't exactly stop then either.

"Okay, fine. You kept me alive. I got to live this life. I appreciate it, but now I want to keep it and you don't care. You claim to want me and need me, but you couldn't care less what I want. It's all very selfish of you. It's all about what Leif wants. You don't take into consideration what I want. You act as if I'm your possession and I should just be happy about it."

She was mine. But I was more hers than she understood. I belonged to her too. She owned me. She just didn't want me. The realization that she was no longer controlling the car had begun to sink in and her heart rate increased, as did her breathing. I was once again scaring her. Damn, I hated this.

"I've tried to make this easy on you. I've tried to make this transition one you could accept. I've sheltered you from the truth. I wanted you to make this decision because you wanted it. Not because I was forcing it upon you, but we've run out of time. There is something you need to know," I pointed to the side of the road before we reached the bridge. I needed to tell her more first, "pull over."

The car immediately parked itself on the side of the road without Pagan's assistance. She'd never truly seen me use my powers. I knew this was more than she was ready to see, but there was no more time.

"What is it I need to know?" She asked slamming her palms down on the steering wheel in frustration.

"You aren't going to like this. I didn't want you to ever know. But when you refused to accept that your soul was the restitution for the life my father granted you, my father decided he'd take his restitution elsewhere." I needed her complete attention. It was time she focused on what I had to say. "Pagan, look at me."

Her head turned and her eyes sparkled with unshed tears as she waited on me to speak. "Wyatt's death was only the beginning. Ghede will take more. Everyone close to you. He'll take them one at a time until you either cave in and agree to come with me or there is no one else left to take."

Shaking her head, she screamed, "No! You are lying. You are a liar. I saw Dank. I saw him draw out Wyatt's soul. Dank would have never taken a soul for your father. He would have never—"

"Dank didn't know. Did he tell you about it beforehand? Did he prepare you for the death of your friend? No. He didn't. Because Wyatt's death wasn't that of fate. My father used his power over your unpaid restitution to kill the body Wyatt's soul inhabited. Dank was drawn there to retrieve the soul from the body because that's his job. He was as surprised as you were."

She knew now. Would she hate me?

"But...but you said my death and Wyatt's death were to be the tragedies this school year. That would mean Wyatt's death was fate."

"I lied to you. I wanted you to be angry at Dank. I could feel your pain and I knew you were staying away from him."

I watched as a range of emotions played across her face. This was so much more than any human mind could comprehend. But she wasn't normal. She'd been seeing souls most of her life. She was in love with Death. Nothing about Pagan was normal. She would be strong enough to deal with this. If only I'd been able to make her fall in love with me first. I'd failed us both.

"Okay. I'll go with you."

I didn't wait for her to think about this any further. While it was her choice, I was taking her. This was it. I started the engine with the snap of my fingers and gunned the gas.

"Leif! Help me!" Pagan screamed as the car raced toward the middle of the bridge. With the swipe of my finger the steering wheel jerked.

"I got you Pagan," I assured her as the car broke through the railing and we went careening out over the ocean waters below us. Vilokan, the afterlife of the Voodoo religion, was located under the sea. I wouldn't apport her this time. It was too hard on her. We would go down the old fashioned way. The dark waters engulfed us and I reached over to force Pagan's body into a deep sleep before pulling her to me and sinking to the depths below. Soon, we'd be home.

11. I can't wait to spend eternity with you- Leif

I couldn't get her to leave my bedroom. She refused to walk around the castle or explore Vilokan with me. Instead, Pagan stayed huddled away in my bedroom where I was no longer welcomed without an invite. Father hadn't exactly made a very good impression on her with his sexual escapades during the one dinner she had attended. Agreeing to let her speak with Wyatt had been the only thing I could think of to make her happy.

Opening the door, Wyatt walked past me without an acknowledgement. He hated me. He hated who I was and what I represented. Once, he'd been my friend. Throughout my life I'd watched him and wished I had a life similar to his. He'd been the friend of Pagan's that intrigued me the most. He had the life of a normal boy.

I'd brought Pagan food that she recognized. The meals my father enjoyed were not something she would accept easily. His appetites were very odd in all things. Setting the tray down on the table beside the bed, I met Pagan's gaze.

"He isn't fond of me," I said as I handed her a plate.

"No, he isn't. But then who can blame him? You took away his eternity. He is now stuck here, forever."

The hate laced in her words was more painful than anything I could have ever imagined. "I didn't take his soul, Pagan, my father did. I had no idea he was going to. Ghede answers to no one within our realm. He makes decisions that please him and he overindulges in anything pleasurable and corrupts enjoyable pursuits, making things that should be good and satisfying into depraved behaviors. Nothing I can say will stop him. I was a child when he asked me to choose a soul. I had no idea what the implications were. I chose you. I didn't know then what that meant. You can hate me, but try to understand I am not my father."

Pagan was quiet a moment and I began fixing a plate of food. "Who is your mother?"

My mother wasn't someone I really wanted to discuss. Ever. But with Pagan I would share everything. Even the painful things. "My mother is Erzulie, she is the reason my skin is pale and my hair is blond. She's the Voodoo Goddess of many things. Love being one...vengeance being another. She takes many lovers and enjoys the same things my father does. I see her on occasion, but for the most part, I live with my father. She has never had any desire for a child, but then I'm not her only one. She has several, many of whom walk the earth. She is not above taking human men to her um...bed."

Pagan took small bites of the pulled pork I'd brought her and I sighed in relief. She needed to eat. I didn't like the idea of her starving. Father would make her immortal soon. But for now, she needed nourishment.

"You don't talk like your father either. He has a bit of a Cajun accent."

Finally, she was curious about me. "I've spent the majority of my life following you. I adopted your accent so I would fit in with your life. I didn't want to appear to you as an outsider."

"So all those dreams I've had are real? Those things really happened. Are there more memories I've forgotten?"

Those were only small tid-bits of our life together. There was so much I wanted her to remember, "Maybe a few more." I replied.

"A few more? That's all?"

I didn't want to hide anything else from her. I'd hid so much already. I set my plate down and stood up. If I was going to tell her this, I needed to be able to pace. It helped me think. Besides, having her perched on my bed made it hard to concentrate on much of anything else. My mind kept going back to the time on her couch, before Dankmar had consumed her heart. I'd never been that close to anyone.

"I've been with you many times in your life. When you were lonely or sad, I was there. When you were in danger, I was there. It was what I did. Father said you were mine and I should protect you. So I did. I'm sorry that you don't remember. It wasn't something I did on purpose. It's just that I am soulless and your soul can't remember me for long when I'm not near you."

"Why did you want me to remember those times? The ones you'd picked out for me to dream about?"

I stopped and turned to stare directly at her. "Because those were the times I fell a little more in love with you."

"You don't love me, Leif. If you loved me, you'd have never been able to hold me against my will."

"I told you I can't control my father. He saved your life. He owns you, Pagan."

"No one owns me."

She didn't understand. I began to fear she never would. "I don't want to argue with you. Not tonight. Let's just eat. Okay?"

I went back to my plate and we ate in silence. When Pagan set her plate down, I did the same. "Are you full?" I asked standing in order to clean up our meal.

"Yes," she mumbled.

I couldn't make her forgive me. Tonight, I'd had all of this I could handle. Turning, I headed for the door to leave her once again, alone. Just before I reached the door, I turned back and tried one more time.

"What can I do to prove to you that I do love you? Anything except letting you go, because I can't. I'll do whatever else you ask of me. I want you to accept this. Us. Just tell me."

She stared back at me without saying anything for a few moments. Then finally she replied. "Release Wyatt to a transporter. Don't keep him here."

Could this be the way to win her heart? "If I can convince my father to release Wyatt to a transporter, then you will believe I love you and you'll let this work between us?"

"Yes, if you hand Wyatt's soul over to a transporter and I get to see this happen. Once I know it has happened and that his soul is where it belongs, then I will do whatever I can to make you happy. To make...us... happy."

We could be happy. I'd make this happen. No matter what I had to do, I'd make this happen. "You have a deal. Get some rest, Pagan. Tomorrow is a new day and I can't wait to start eternity with you."

12. I CAN GET YOU BOTH OUT OF HERE...ALIVE- LEIF

Father wasn't going to be easy to convince when it came to letting Wyatt's soul go to Dankmar. He hated the power Dankmar held over him. In Vilokan, Father held the power. However, Dankmar held the power over the souls of creation. But I needed Pagan's forgiveness. My future had been planned out with her from the time I was a boy. I couldn't let that go. I didn't want to watch her hate for me grow each day.

"Excuse me, but I need to find someone and I am completely lost. Do you know Rosella, red hair...and hopefully still alive? I thought maybe that might stand out here, ya know."

Stopping, I turned to find an attractive petite girl around my age coming from the main entrance. First thing I noticed other than the fact she had really big brown eyes and incredibly long eyelashes was the fact she was wearing clothes. Normal clothes. Her jeans were worn and faded, but hugged her thin hips nicely. The black tee shirt she was wearing had, "Don't make me go Cajun on your ass," written across it in white block letters. Nothing about this girl looked Cajun. Her pale skin and coppery colored hair screamed Irish.

"Hey, are you, like, alive, too? Because you look like it, but then it's hard to tell here," she asked. I lifted my eyes from her shirt and met her gaze. The pink in her cheeks and beat of her heart told me she was in fact a human. What was my father thinking? Was he collecting a whole horde of humans? Then the thought of why he would have collected another human washed over me. Oh, fuck no. She was my age!

"Who are you and how did you get here?" I asked studying her for any sign of a lie.

Her posture straightened and the openly curious expression she'd been aiming at me darkened. Great, I'd pissed off yet another female. "I'm Sabine Monroe. I'm looking for my sister. Rosella Monroe. She's older than me. Same hair," she paused and pressed her lips together firmly. Something was upsetting her and I was positive it wasn't my rude behavior. "Hopefully, still alive."

"You're alive," I stated.

Sabine nodded slowly like maybe she needed to find someone else with a little more sense.

"How did you get here? This is the Voodoo *afterlife*. It isn't normal to see a living, breathing human walking the halls. Typically, it's the souls of those who served Ghede who enter Vilokan."

Sabine put her hands on her hips and sighed. I noticed her nails were neatly filed and each white tip had a black Fleur De Lis on the end. "I'm aware of where I am. Obviously, the living and breathing can enter the walls of Vilokan if they know what they're doing. Trust me, I don't want to be here. I just need someone to tell me where I can find my sister so that I can take her home. Back to the surface where we can continue living and breathing and staying the hell away from my Mamé's Voodoo crap."

"Okay, wait. Your sister is here and you are looking for her. Both of you are alive? You're not a Voodoo queen heir or a witch, but you are here. Where only those Ghede allows to enter may walk."

A small shiver ran over her and she shook her head, "No, I'm none of those things. My Mamé, however, needs a good lesson in messing with the Voodoo junk she buys from the shop on Bourbon. I've told her that mess wasn't something to screw around with. But no one listens to the eighteen-year-old. So, here I am."

The red-headed female whom I'd seen with my father months ago. Surely that wasn't who this girl was after. But, who else? The red hair was similar. Maybe. I hadn't paid enough attention to the girl with Father. I'd been worried about Dankmar taking Pagan from me. This girl did not need to meet my father. His taste in females could be disturbing. The idea of him using this girl sickened me. She was too young, too innocent, too…beautiful. Not to mention, I needed to get Father to agree to letting Wyatt's soul go back to Dankmar.

"Listen, I have some stuff I have to deal with tonight. I can find your sister. But you're in a dangerous place. Ghede, he is the—"

"Voodoo lord of the dead. Yeah, I know. My Mamé explained all that before she sent me to the old Voodoo witch who in return sent me here."

"Right. Okay, well, he isn't exactly a nice understanding guy. If you could give me a day to work some things out and let me find your sister, I'll bring her to you, then I'll get you both out of here."

Sabine cocked one eyebrow, "Yeah, you? And how will you do that? With your good looks? Because God knows you aren't a Voodoo spirit. You look as human as I do."

I had to bite back a laugh, which was surprising. I hadn't been much in the mood for laughter earlier. "Listen, Sabine. I can promise you I've got connections. Just please do as I say and wait for me. I'm the only one who has a chance at getting you both out of here…*alive.*"

13. Let her go- Leif

I knocked once then opened the door, "It's time," I announced as I made my way into the bedroom. Pagan had been given a chance to say her goodbyes to Wyatt. A transporter had been alerted of Wyatt's return. Everything was set in place. Soon, I'd have the eternity I'd always imagined with Pagan.

She pulled on the short length of the black dress Father had supplied for her to wear. It was his way of showing Dankmar just who Pagan belonged to now. I knew she hated the flimsiness of the dress, but I'd managed to get Father to agree to so much already, I wasn't about to argue with him on this one.

"Let's do this," she replied making her way to the door. Thankful that she wasn't going to put up a fight, I held out my arm to escort her, but she backed away and shook her head, "No, it's not over yet. You get Wyatt safely in a transporter's hands and out of this place, then I'll hold up my end of the deal."

She was stubborn, but I wasn't going to argue. Instead, I nodded my head.

"You lead the way," she said once we were in the hallway.

"You know that Dankmar will probably be here, Pagan."

"I figure he would be."

"You understand the implications if you go to him."

"Yes, Leif, I know you'll kill off everyone I love and suck their souls down here to live in fornication for all eternity. Got it."

I loved her so fiercely, but she could make me so angry. "Pagan, this isn't about me. I've told you this is all my father. It's how he operates. I can't control him. You have no idea how much cajoling I had to do in order for him to give Wyatt's soul back. And to be honest, the only reason I think he agreed is because he sees entertainment value in you refusing to go to Dankmar and that he will be the one controlling you."

I noticed the door across the hall. It opened slightly and two large brown eyes peered out. The wide-eyed expression on Sabine's face told me she had heard quite a bit of the argument Pagan and I were having. I had to focus on my problem at hand. I'd deal with Sabine and her sister later.

"Now, please understand, no pain you have suffered is because I wanted it. I never wanted you to hurt. I always thought you'd want me. That your soul would want me. Hell, when I get anywhere near you, your eyes look like they've caught on fire. You're supposed to want me. But you don't. Instead you want him. And you can't have him, Pagan. It was never meant to be."

"Okay," was her simple reply.

"Okay?"

"You heard me, Leif. I said okay. Now, let's go."

Well, that was easier than I'd expected. With one last glance in Sabine's nosy direction, I turned and made my way to the front entrance.

"Stop it," I growled at one of the Voodoo spirits as they gawked at Pagan's body in the dress Father had made her wear.

"May, dat is sumtin to see, is it not?" Father called out as he walked into the large foyer.

"Don't make her uncomfortable, Father," I pleaded.

"Who, me?" he asked in an amused voice. I watched as he lifted his hand and placed two cigarettes in his mouth and then turned his attention to the activities going on outside.

I searched the onlookers for any sight of Sabine's sister. If I could find her now, then once this was over, I could help Sabine and her sister escape. Then, it would be time to enjoy my forever with Pagan. That is, *if* we all survived Death's fury.

"Please, make them stop," Pagan whispered desperately. Confused, I looked down at her then followed her gaze to see two women from Father's harem running their fingers over Wyatt's crotch. Most teenage guys would enjoy that, but I could see that Wyatt was uncomfortable and Pagan was very upset over it. But Wyatt had figured out complaining would only encourage Father.

"If I make a scene, Father will then make it much worse. If you don't want to see one of those two mount Wyatt right here, then don't say a word. Wyatt knows this. That's why he's so still."

Silence fell over the wild streets and people began fleeing. All the laughter and drinking ended as souls felt the presence of Death closing in on them.

"Ah, Death draws near. The fallen 'ave run to hide," Father drawled and pulled the two cigarettes from his mouth to exhale small rings of smoke before placing them right back in.

"What does he mean?" Pagan asked.

"Dank is close. The souls of the people in the streets felt him and ran. Unlike you, most humans don't cling to Death when he's in his true form. Sure, they like the singer Dank Walker, but when he's truly in Death's form, they hide."

Father turned to Wyatt and crooked his finger once. The girls holding onto him released their claim on him as he stepped forward.

Gasps turned my attention to the streets in front of me. Dankmar had come and he hadn't come alone. Death's eyes searched until they found Pagan, who I had cuddled up against my side. She was mine.

"Well, well, well, Dankmar and pals. To wat do we owe dis honor?" Father asked in his usual jolly tone.

"You know why I'm here, Ghede," Dankmar replied not taking his eyes off of Pagan. The possessive gleam in his eyes made my skin crawl in fear. Would I be able to stand up to him? Would Father expect me to handle Dankmar all on my own?

"Tsk tsk tsk, I don know whut you mean. You said to let her choose," Father announced waving his hand in our direction. "She did."

The blonde transporter started toward us when Dankmar stopped her. Did he not plan on taking her? Would it really be this easy?

"No. You forced her choice. That wasn't part of the deal," Dankmar roared. Pagan shivered in my arms and stepped back away from me.

"Here's the soul you came for," Father pushed Wyatt toward Death and instantly Wyatt was in the protection of a transporter's arms. Then he was gone. Pagan had gotten her wish, her one demand. It had been fulfilled. Now, Death needed to leave.

"Now, is dat all you want or would you lak to axe her yorself?" Father turned toward us, "Come here, Pagan," he coaxed.

She was terrified of Father. I gently squeezed her arm in reassurance, then nudged her forward. She had to go to him. If she refused him, everything could get ugly.

"Axe her, Dankmar," Father cackled as he grabbed Pagan and shoved her toward Death.

I took a step toward her. What was Father thinking? Dankmar could reach out and take her.

"I want—"

"I didn't ask you anything just yet, Pagan. Hold onto that thought just a moment more," Dankmar instructed lifting his gaze from Pagan to focus on Father. "You've messed with the wrong guy this time, Ghede. You like your entertainment, but I was never one to entertain."

The transporters began to move away from Dankmar. Were they all getting ready to leave? Was this finally over? Then the warriors began to descend. I'd never seen one of the Creator's warriors before. I'd heard of them. Feared them. But never had I seen them. The massive swords that hung on their side would simply wipe out our world with a single swipe. A human's freewill was the only power we held. The warriors, however, were given their power from the actual Creator. We had no chance against them.

"You brought de warriors for a gurl?" Father asked in astonishment.

"Yes," Dankmar replied, then took a step forward holding his hand out to Pagan.

"I can't," she sobbed.

"Trust me," he replied. I waited knowing that this was it. If she went to him, I would let her go. I would give up. If Pagan chose him one more time, then I would let her go.

As if in slow motion, Pagan stepped forward and placed her hand in his. Dankmar pulled her up against his side tightly. The relief on his face was mirrored in her eyes as she gazed up at him. He was where she wanted to be. I couldn't fight this anymore. All I was doing was making her hate me even more every passing day. I'd loved Pagan for the majority of my life, but I couldn't force her to love me. I finally understood that.

"Bad choice, leetle gurl," Father hissed. He hadn't expected her to go. Deep down, I'd known she would.

"No, Ghede. You're the only one who made a bad choice. You don't take what's mine." Dankmar challenged. Then he paused and bent down to whisper in Pagan's ear before handing her to the blonde transporter that had so fiercely protected Pagan before.

"You took a soul that was too young to defend itself. A soul that belonged to the Creator. You changed fate and then decided to play with a world that is not yours. You stepped out of your realm and took another soul not under your rule. Now, I give you a choice, Ghede. We close this portal today as well as the ones found in Africa and Haiti where the warriors are now standing guard, and we seal them for all eternity. Voodoo power will end right here. Right now. You crossed a line." The gauntlet had been thrown. Dankmar held the power.

"Or you let Pagan's soul go. Free of any restitution. You stay clear of her and her family for all eternity and remain as you are. But I warn you, if I see your son, you or any of your spirits again remotely close to Pagan again, I will end this religion. There will be no second chances. It's your choice."

Father turned and stared back at me. I could feel his eyes boring into me as I studied Pagan. This was it. I would have to let her go now. It was the only way. She was never meant to be mine. Even though in my heart, she always would be.

"Let her go." I replied. Then I dropped my eyes from her gaze and turned to walk away. Back into the castle, where my future would never be complete. I'd lost the only key to my happiness.

14. I'm nothing like my Father- Leif

A mix of emotions churned violently inside me. I couldn't decide if despair, anger, loss, or hate was the most powerful. How had I failed so easily? Why hadn't I moved in sooner and won her heart?

"Um, hey, you…uh, Leif, I think," a familiar voice broke into my inner turmoil and I jerked my head around to glare at the intruder when I met the startled expression of Sabine. I'd forgotten about her. Shit. I wasn't in the frame of mind to help anyone right now. Someone needed to help me.

"Oh my. Um, I take it things didn't go so well with the girl," she said softly.

"Obvious, is it?" I snapped.

Her big brown eyes widened. "I'm sorry."

The sincerity in her voice was my undoing. The emotions inside me all stepped back to let sorrow take the leading role as tears filled my eyes.

"She didn't choose me," I managed to say without chocking up.

"Oh. Wow. Well, uh, maybe that is for the…best?"

I wanted to roar that it wasn't for the best. It would never be for the best. How could the fact I'd lost everything important to me ever be for the best? Stalking toward my bedroom without replying, I stopped and touched the cold doorknob, then paused. Her scent would be in there. Her clothes. My pillow would smell of her. I'd see her there on my bed. I wasn't that strong yet. Instead, I turned and walked back to the room I'd been sleeping in since Pagan had been here.

Sabine still stood in the hallway watching me anxiously. I knew she wanted my help, but right now, I couldn't bring myself to care.

"You could come in and talk about it. If that would help," Sabine paused and wrung her hands, "it always helps me to talk about things and I'm a really good listener."

Damn, she was nice. I didn't need to be around nice right now. I was anything but nice at the moment. "No, thanks. I need to be alone," I replied as politely as I could manage before opening the door to my temporary room.

"If you go in that room, I will find my sister alone. I'm sorry that you're upset, but I'm not standing around and waiting for you any longer. I need to find Rosella. She's been gone too long already. I'm in a hurry."

Telling Sabine to go ahead and try was so tempting. The only thing that kept me from walking away from her was the fact she would never make it out of here alive. I was the only chance she had. Those damn big innocent eyes of hers were pulling on my human side. The part of me that felt compassion and remorse, the part that had been molded by my love for Pagan.

"Fine, I'll help you. But I'm not in the mood for a hassle. Listen to me. Do what I say and we will get along just fine. Understood?

"Yeah, captain, I got it." She drawled in a sexy southern accent I hadn't paid much attention to earlier.

Nodding, my thoughts went back to Pagan. Was she happy now? What was she doing? Would she miss me at all?

I needed to see her one last time. Could I get away with going to check on her or would Dankmar make good on his threat? Forcing thoughts of Pagan aside, I focused on the girl standing in front of me. The one who needed me.

"I'll go find your sister now. You stay here in your room."

Sabine began shaking her head.

"That part isn't up for discussion. I will bring your sister back to you. But if you go with me, it will mess up everything. Ghede isn't going to just let you walk away from here if he sees you."

She swallowed nervously, "You mean your father?"

So, she had heard a lot more of mine and Pagan's conversation than I'd realized. "Yeah, my father."

Finally, she stepped back into her room and started to close the door. I watched as she studied me a moment. "But you didn't make the girl stay with you. She wanted to leave and you let her."

"I'm not my father. I'm nothing like my father. That's the problem."

"Closer" by Dank Walker

"Daylight fades away as I watch you from a distance
Darkness claims the sky and I wish you could only know
We're supposed to be miles away, but something draws me closer
We're supposed to be far away, but gravity brings us closer
Closer than your skin, rebellion deep within, you've taken over me and
I can't seem to swim. To the top of myself, I'm under your control. I'm
wondering how we got here I'm wondering how we got here to the place we
should go.
Ooooh oooh oooooh
The place we should go
Ooooh ooooooh ooooh
Souls aren't meant for things like this
Our worlds were never meant to collide
You're better off leaving while you have something to leave behind
We're supposed to be miles away, but something draws me closer
We're supposed to be far away, but gravity beings us closer
Closer than your skin, rebellion deep within, you've taken over me and
I can't seem to swim. To the top of myself, I'm under your control. I'm
wondering how we got here I'm wondering how we got here to the place we
should go.
We're supposed to be miles away, but something draws me closer."

You can hear the original song here: https://soundcloud.com/abbi-glines/closer

ABOUT THE AUTHOR

Abbi Glines is a *#1 New York Times*, *USA Today*, and *Wall Street Journal* bestselling author of the Rosemary Beach, Sea Breeze, Vincent Boys, and Existence series. She has a new YA series coming out in the fall of 2015 titled The Field Party Series. She never cooks unless baking during the Christmas holiday counts. She believes in ghosts and has a habit of asking people if their house is haunted before she goes in it. She drinks afternoon tea because she wants to be British but alas she was born in Alabama. When asked how many books she has written she has to stop and count on her fingers. When she's not locked away writing, she is reading, shopping (major shoe and purse addiction), sneaking off to the movies alone, and listening to the drama in her teenagers lives while making mental notes on the good stuff to use later. *Don't judge.*

You can connect with Abbi online in several different ways. She uses social media to procrastinate.

Facebook *facebook.com/AbbiGlinesAuthor*

Website *AbbiGlines.com*

Twitter https://twitter.com/AbbiGlines

Instagram: abbiglines

Snapchat: abbiglines

13398509R00046

Printed in Great Britain
by Amazon.co.uk, Ltd.,
Marston Gate.